Home Tweet

MW01103921

Written by Della Bartzen

Illustrated by Lizy J Campbell

Published by

4Paws
Games and
Publishing

Bruno, Saskatchewan, Canada

Home Tweet Home
Written by Della Bartzen
Illustrations and Cover Art by Lizy J Campbell
Edited by 4 Paws Games and Publishing
Formatted and Published by 4 Paws Games and Publishing
Published 2019 First Edition
ISBN 13: 978-1-988345-98-7

Published by 4 Paws Games and Publishing
P.O. Box 444 Humboldt, Saskatchewan, Canada S0K 2A0
http://www.4-Paws-Games-and-Publishing.ca

Dedication

I would like to dedicate this book to my Dad, Henry Wedhorn, and to my twin sister Ella Nancy Wedhorn...you may be gone from this earth but will never be gone from my heart.

So Jesus said to him, "Unless you people see signs and wonders, you simply will not believe." (John 4:48)

A little girl Ella Nancy had a true story she wanted to tell.

It started out a sad tale but ended up quite well.

Now Ella she had four pets if you can imagine that. A green bird named Kiwi, a yellow one named Lemonade, a dog plus a cat.

One afternoon Ella and her birds all settled for a nap, along with Cooler the brown dog and Mitzy the black-white cat.

When Ella heard a sudden crash, she ran outside to see,

that's when Lemonade flew from her arm and into Mr. Wedhorn's tree.

Ella stood in disbelief and did not make a sound,

as Lemonade soared like an eagle and did not touch the ground.

Lemonade would not land but Ella she stayed calm,

she would catch her in the morning at the crack of dawn.

But the next day a tornado blew, the skies they turned to grey,

and Ella, she worried that Lemonade would blow away.

The following day it was sunny out and oh so very hot.

Ella wondered would Lemonade find water to drink or not.

The third day it rained and poured cats and dogs they'd say,

and Ella hoped that Lemonade would find a dry place to stay.

A week had passed, and everyone was sad and feeling down.

Kiwi chirped, and Ella feared that Lemonade would not be found!

Now Lemonade was having quite an adventure of her own,

but was starting to get tired and couldn't find her own way home.

Lemonade saw a semi driver and knew just what to do.

She flew and landed on his shoulder and chirped a song or two.

The semi driver was very shocked to have a bird fly on his arm and decided he would take the bird to the veterinary farm.

A young lady volunteering at the vet farm happened to say,

her dad Mr. Wedhorn had told a story of a bird that flew away.

So, Mr. Wedhorn's daughter starting walking door to door,

in hopes that she would find the house where Lemonade had lived before.

When she finally found Ella's house and told her the good news,

Ella simply could not believe just how far Lemonade had flew.

Ella quickly left to get Lemonade from the veterinary farm,

and cuddled and placed her precious bird back on her forearm.

Then Ella took Lemonade home for all the pets to see,

and they talked in their pet language and were as happy as could be.

Although Ella wondered about Lemonade's adventures while being on her own,

all Ella really cared about now was Lemonade was ... Home TWEET Home.

The Real Animals

1 LEMONADE AND KIWI

2 Cooler

3 MITZY

About the Author

Della Bartzen (Wedhorn) was born and raised in Morse, Saskatchewan and now lives in Moose Jaw, Saskatchewan. Della has been married for 32 years, is mother of two adult boys and recently became a first time Grandma to a beautiful Granddaughter.

Working as a Licensed Practical Nurse (LPN), and a Public Protection Complaints Investigator, Della is also trained as a Mediator and holds designation as a Qualified Arbitrator (Q.ARB). Della is extremely excited and feels very fortunate to add "Children's Book Author" to her portfolio.

Although Della always had a lifelong love for children's books and a dream of writing her own book one day, she just wasn't convinced that she had an exciting enough story to write about. However, after her precious tiny parrotlet Lemonade, flew away, was gone for a week and then by some miracle safely returned into her arms, Della immediately knew this unbelievable but true story needed to be published for all to enjoy!

Believing in "what's meant to be will be," Della is extremely excited to see her book come to fruition and hopes everyone will enjoy this true story as much as she enjoyed writing it!!

Made in the USA
Monee, IL
17 February 2020